Book 1

learn to play the baritone b.c.!

A carefully graded method
that emphasizes good tone production,
builds a sound rhythmic sense and
develops well-rounded musicianship.

by Charles F. Gouse

GETTING ACQUAINTED WITH MUSIC

NOTES are musical sounds indicated by symbols. Their *time length* is shown by their color (white or black) and by stems and flags attached to the note:

Notes are named after the first seven letters of the alphabet (A to G) and are repeated to include the entire range of musical sound.

THE STAFF is five horizontal lines and the spaces between. The *name* and *pitch* of the note is determined by its position on the staff. When notes go above or below the staff, *leger lines* are used.

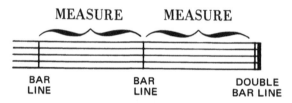

MEASURES divide music into equal parts. A *bar line* separates one measure from another. A *double bar line* shows where the music ends.

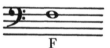

THE BASS CLEF (or F clef) is a sign which locates F on the staff. From that F, all other notes can be named and located.

TIME SIGNATURES indicate the *number* of beats (or counts) in each measure (upper number). It also tells the *kind* of note that receives *one* beat (lower number). The first *time signature* used in this book is:

$$\frac{4}{4} = \begin{array}{l} \text{4 beats to each measure} \\ \text{a quarter note (} \quarternote \text{) receives 1 beat} \end{array}$$

ACCIDENTALS are marks placed before notes which alter their original pitch. A *flat* (♭) lowers a note one half-step, a *sharp* (♯) raises a note one half-step. and a *natural* (♮) restores a note to its original pitch.

GETTING ACQUAINTED
WITH YOUR INSTRUMENT

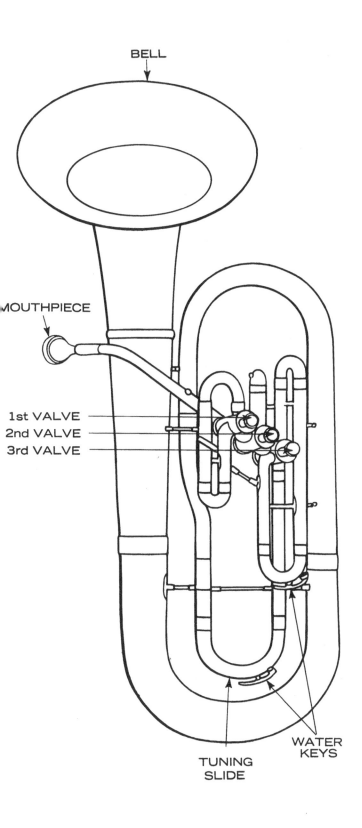

BELL

MOUTHPIECE

1st VALVE

2nd VALVE

3rd VALVE

WATER
KEYS

TUNING
SLIDE

LEFT HAND: Hold the instrument as shown above. Your teacher may suggest a different position for your left hand depending on your size.

RIGHT HAND: Place the thumb of your right hand between the 1st and 2nd valve casings. Place the tips of your fingers on the valve tops. Make sure you arch your fingers. Do not let them cave in. Your pinky position will depend on the size of your hand. Your teacher will help you.

GETTING READY TO PLAY

1.

2.

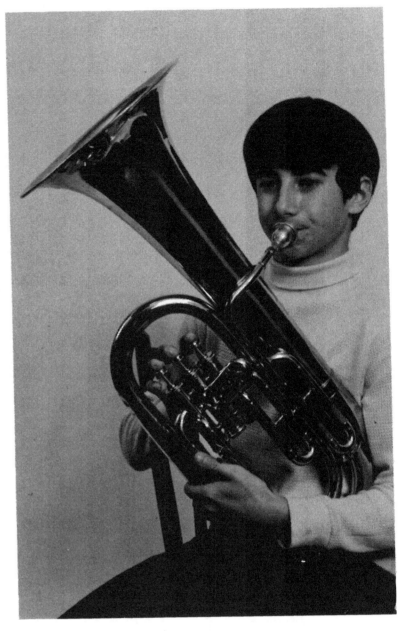

3.

1. Look at the photographs above. Form your lips as shown in photo No. 1. Keep your lips stretched firmly against your teeth. Take a large breath at the corners of your mouth. *Do not raise your chest or shoulders.* Push the air out between your lips. Try to produce a "BUZZING" sound. This "BUZZ" is a vibration that will cause the instrument to play.

2. When you have succeeded in making the BUZZ, place the mouthpiece on your lips as shown in photo No. 2. Your teacher will help you place it approximately 1/3 on the upper lip and 2/3 on the bottom. Take a breath as before. Make sure your breath is deep. Try to BUZZ through the mouthpiece. Listen for a sound that is like a QUACK.

3. To help start the BUZZ cleanly: Take your breath as before. This time hold the air back with the tip of your tongue, which is placed on the back edge of your upper teeth. When you are ready to start the tone, drop the tip of the tongue as though you were saying the letter T. The BUZZ should start immediately. This is called *tonguing* or *attacking* a note.

4. Rest a bit after each BUZZ, and while you are resting look at photo No. 3. Also review the holding of your instrument. Now, put the mouthpiece in the instrument and place it on your lips again. Do not depress any values. Take your breath, tongue and blow. Most likely you will produce a musical tone. Probably it will be one of the following three notes:

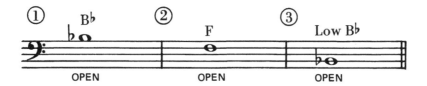

YOUR TEACHER WILL TELL YOU WHICH ONE YOU PLAYED.

5. Your goal is to play F. If you played the higher B♭(1), relax the corners of your lips and form your mouth as though you were saying TAH. If you played the lower B♭(3), tighten the corners of your mouth and form the word TEE.

6. When you can tongue and blow F accurately, see how long you can sustain the tone. Don't force it. Let the BUZZ and the breath do the work for you. Try to play a full, strong tone that sounds pretty.

7. This mark ⌢ is a Fermata. It is a *hold* sign. When placed over a note, it means to hold the note longer than usual.

YOU ARE NOW READY TO PLAY

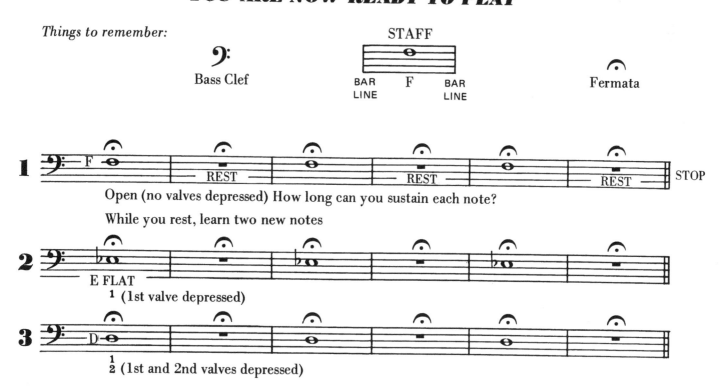

WHOLE NOTES AND WHOLE RESTS

In $\frac{4}{4}$ time, there are four beats (or counts) in each measure. A *whole note* (○) receives all four beats. $\frac{4}{4}$ may also be written as **C**. This stands for *Common Time*.

In No. 1, start by counting aloud, "1—2—3—4". Count *steadily*. Now tap your foot *very lightly* and *think* the count. If you can tap, think and play the notes, you are well on your way towards becoming a good reader.

Whole note ○ = 4 counts (or beats)   Whole rest 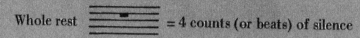 = 4 counts (or beats) of silence

HALF NOTES AND HALF RESTS

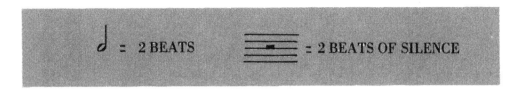

$\half$ = 2 BEATS $\blacksquare$ = 2 BEATS OF SILENCE

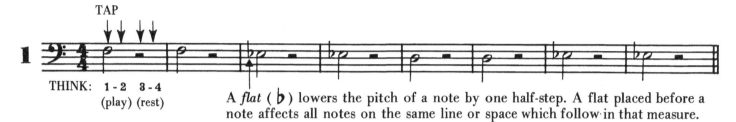

1

TAP

THINK: 1 - 2   3 - 4
         (play) (rest)

A *flat* (♭) lowers the pitch of a note by one half-step. A flat placed before a note affects all notes on the same line or space which follow in that measure.

2

3

4

MIXING WHOLE NOTES AND HALF NOTES

5

6

7

FIRST DUET
(A DUET IS A COMPOSITION FOR TWO PLAYERS)

Player No. 1

8   Always learn both parts of every duet.

Player No. 2

QUARTER NOTES AND QUARTER RESTS

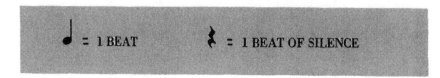

FINGER BUSTER NO. 1

Make sure your valves are fully depressed. Play several times.

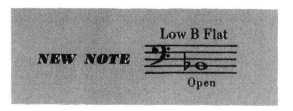

NEW NOTE — Low B Flat / Open

As you go lower, form your mouth as though you were saying TAH.

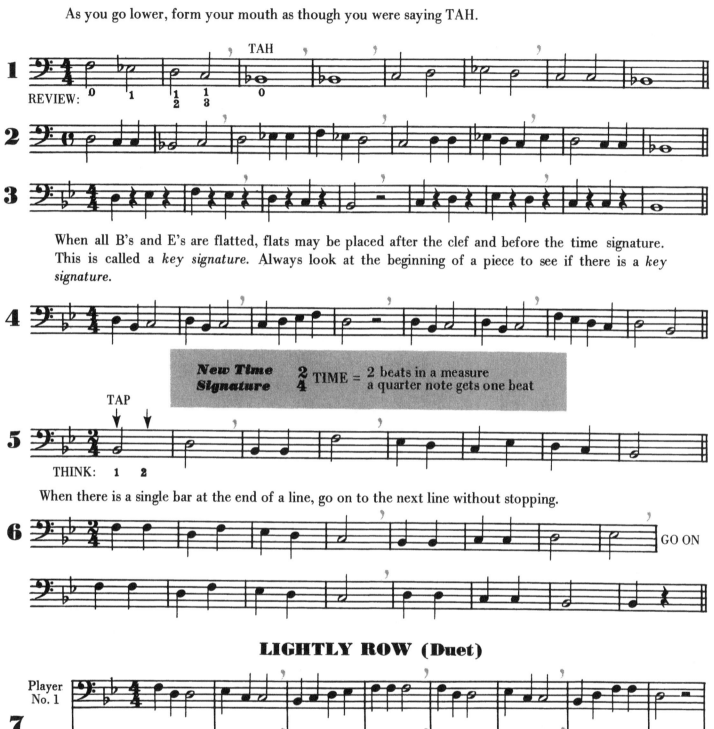

1 REVIEW: TAH

When all B's and E's are flatted, flats may be placed after the clef and before the time signature. This is called a *key signature*. Always look at the beginning of a piece to see if there is a *key signature*.

New Time Signature	$\frac{2}{4}$ TIME	= 2 beats in a measure
		a quarter note gets one beat

5 TAP

THINK: 1   2

When there is a single bar at the end of a line, go on to the next line without stopping.

6 GO ON

LIGHTLY ROW (Duet)

7 Player No. 1 / Player No. 2

No. 1 / No. 2

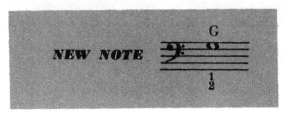

NEW NOTE — G

As you go higher, tighten the corners of your lips and form the inside of your mouth as though you were saying TEE.

1

2

LONDON BRIDGE

3

A *tie* is a curved line that connects two notes of the same pitch. The tone is to be held for the sum of the connected notes.

= 3 BEATS

2 + 1

The tie can come within a measure or it can cross the bar line into the following measure.

TAP

4

THINK: 1 -(2 - 3) 4

HOW MANY BEATS?

5

A *dot* after a note lengthens the note by half of its regular value.

= 3 BEATS

TAP

6

THINK: 1 (2 3) 4

TAP

7

THINK: 1 (2 3) 4

SIX FOLK TUNES WITH SIX NOTES

GO TELL AUNT RHODIE
AMERICAN

AU CLAIRE DE LA LUNE
FRENCH

SCHLAF KINDLEIN, SCHLAF
GERMAN

OATS, PEAS, BEANS
ENGLISH

OLD MAC DONALD
AMERICAN

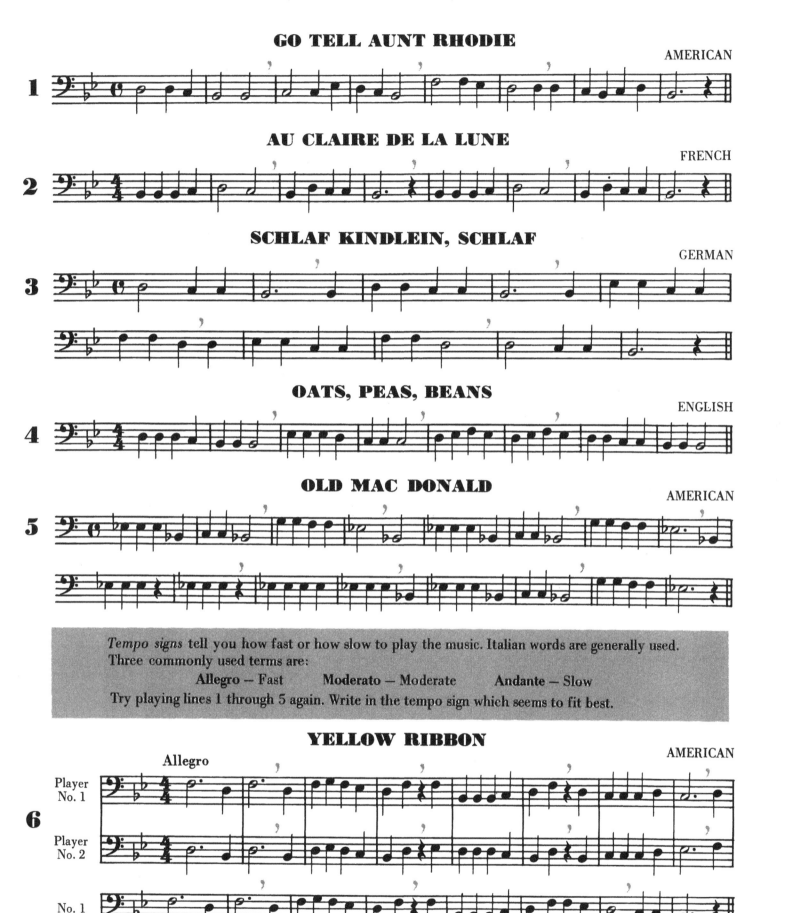

Tempo signs tell you how fast or how slow to play the music. Italian words are generally used. Three commonly used terms are:

Allegro — Fast   **Moderato** — Moderate   **Andante** — Slow

Try playing lines 1 through 5 again. Write in the tempo sign which seems to fit best.

YELLOW RIBBON
AMERICAN

Allegro

Player No. 1

Player No. 2

No. 1

No. 2

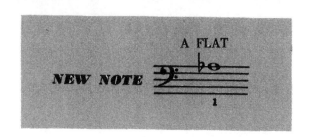

NEW NOTE — A FLAT

1. A FLAT / ALSO A FLAT

2.

LIP BUILDER NO. 1

Listen carefully to the skips between the notes.   Repeat several times

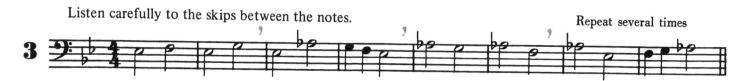

3.

GRADUATION MARCH

Notice that there are three flats in this key signature; B, E and A.

Andante

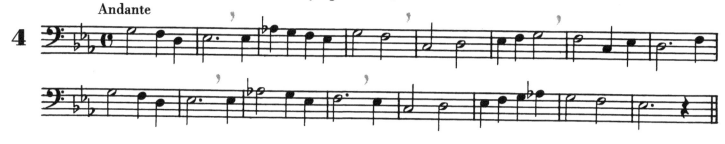

4.

HUSH LITTLE BABY

Moderato

5.

YANKEE DOODLE

Allegro

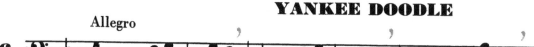

6.

DUET

Moderato

Player No. 1

Player No. 2

7.

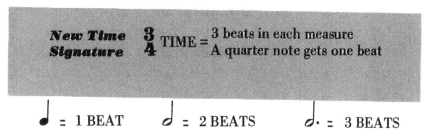

New Time Signature $\frac{3}{4}$ TIME = 3 beats in each measure / A quarter note gets one beat

♩ = 1 BEAT   ♩ = 2 BEATS   ♩. = 3 BEATS

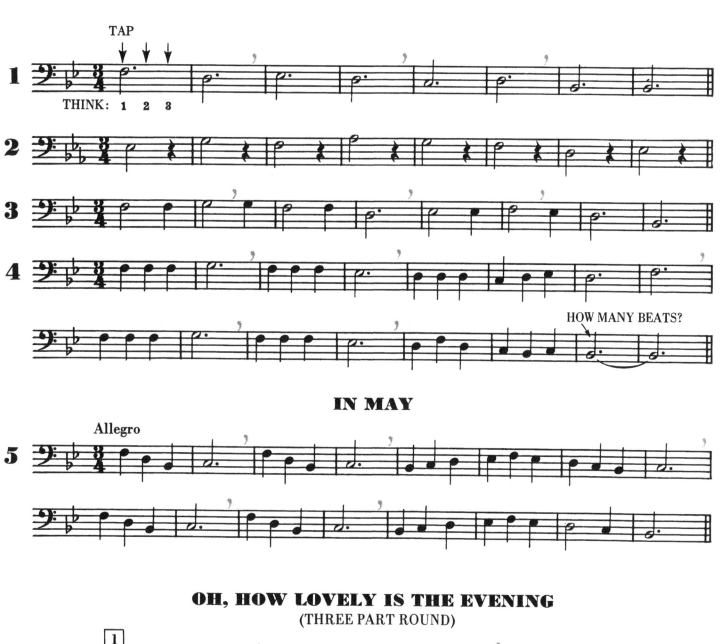

TAP

THINK: 1 2 3

1

2

3

4

HOW MANY BEATS?

IN MAY

Allegro

5

OH, HOW LOVELY IS THE EVENING
(THREE PART ROUND)

6

1

2

3

1st PLAYER — Starts at [1] and plays to the end.

2nd PLAYER — Starts at [1] when first player reaches [2] and plays to the end.

3rd PLAYER — Starts at [1] when second player reaches [2] and plays to the end.

SLURS

A *slur* is a curved line that connect notes of a *different* pitch. The first note is tongued, but the other note (or notes) are not. Valve movements should be quick and smooth.

Breathe where marked. If no breath marks are shown, put them in. Breathe so the flow of the music is not interrupted.

Make sure that your valves are fully depressed.

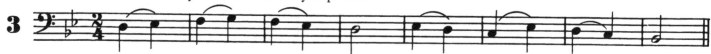

HAPPINESS IS A SMOOTH SLUR

Moderato

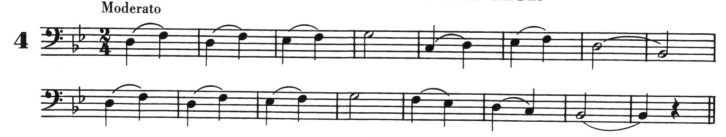

JINGLE BELLS

Allegro

OLD JOE CLARK

Allegro

Slurs can also be played between notes that have the same fingerings. They are called *lip slurs*, and are very important in developing good tone quality and endurance. Imagine you are saying TOO and changing it to AH on the lower note. Frown just a little at the corners of your lips. Do not let your lips sag in the middle, however.

LIP BUILDER NO. 2

Andante   Repeat several times

THINK : Too - Ah   etc.

MORE SLURS

HYMN

FLEMMING

REST AWHILE

A flat, not in the key signature, is called an *accidental*.

THREE NOTE SLURS

THREE NOTES
ARE SLURRED

WATCH OUT

SLURRING PAST (Duet)

NEW NOTES A natural and B flat

When going higher, tighten the corners of your lips. Form your mouth as though you were saying TEE. Do not force the tone.

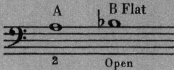

1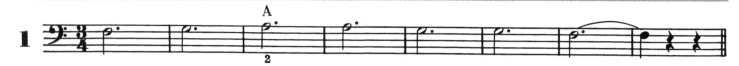

MERRILY WE ROLL ALONG

2

SLURRING TO Bb

3

LIP BUILDER NO. 3

4

FINGER BUSTER NO. 2

Play this three times: 1. Andante   2. Moderato   3. Allegro

5

CAMPTOWN RACES

S. FOSTER

6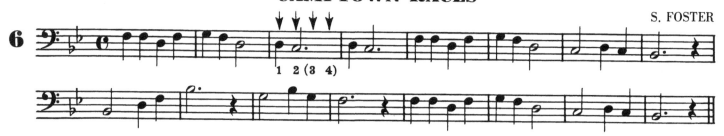

THERE'S A HOLE IN THE BUCKET

7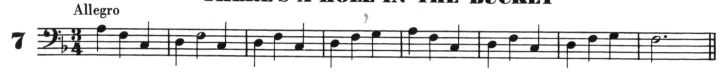

DUKE STREET

This duet has both parts on one staff. The 1st player plays the notes whose stems go up. The 2nd player plays those notes whose stems go down.

8

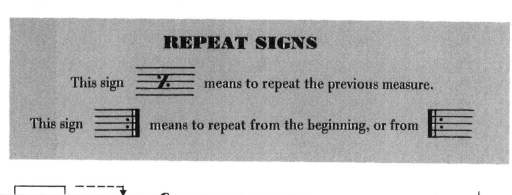

1

STAR GAZER

MOZART

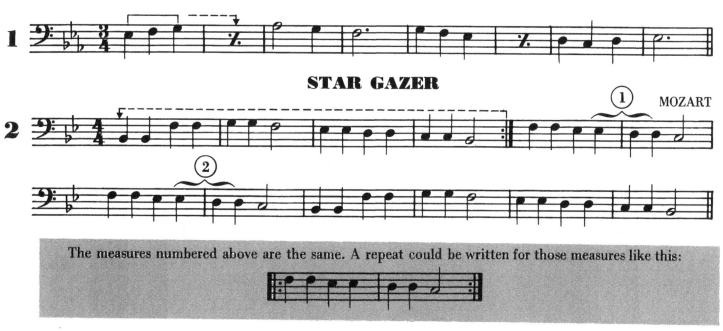

FOX, YOU STOLE THE GOOSE

GERMAN FOLK TUNE

Allegro

3

SLURRING FOUR NOTES

4

OH, SUSANNA (Duet)

Allegro

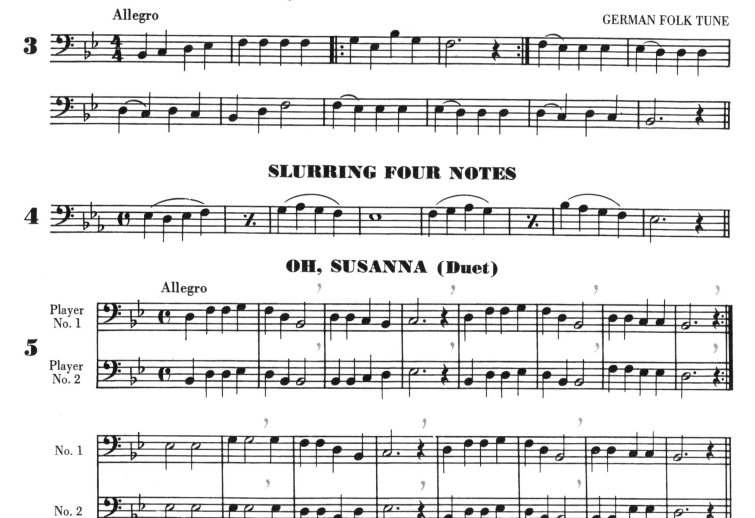

Player No. 1

Player No. 2

5

No. 1

No. 2

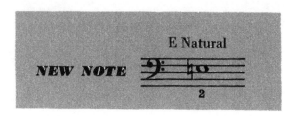

NEW NOTE — E Natural

A *natural* (♮) cancels a sharp or flat and restores a note to its original pitch.

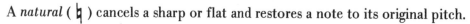

CUCKOO

Notice that there are no flats in the key signature.

SONG FOR AN AUTUMN DAY

THE KING'S PARADE

Notice that there is only one flat (B♭) in the key signature.

THE SLIDER

A LITTLE HARMONY (Duet)

INCOMPLETE MEASURES

Not all music begins on the 1st beat of the measure. The beats missing from the incomplete measure are found in the last measure of the piece. Think and tap the beats that would come before the 1st note or notes. The notes in the incomplete measure are called *pick-up* notes.

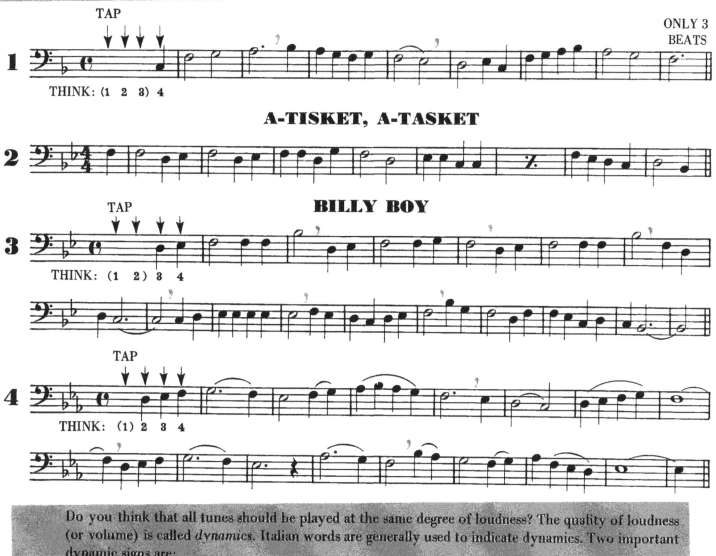

A-TISKET, A-TASKET

BILLY BOY

Do you think that all tunes should be played at the same degree of loudness? The quality of loudness (or volume) is called *dynamics*. Italian words are generally used to indicate dynamics. Two important dynamic signs are:

Piano (*p*) = Soft   Forte (*f*) = Loud

Try playing lines 1 through 4 again. Write in the abbreviation for the dynamic sign which seems correct. Also review some earlier songs and play them using dynamics.

ECHO WALTZ

* *f - p* means to play *forte* the 1st time and *piano* on the repeat.

SCALES

A *scale* is a succession of eight tones. There is either a *half* step or a *whole* step between each note. Every major scale has the same arrangement of steps. Here is the formula:

THE Bb MAJOR SCALE

½ = one half step

1 = whole step

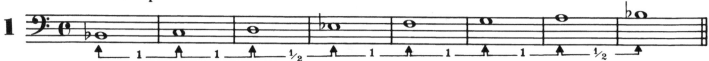

Memorize the Bb scale. Play it in half and quarter notes as well. Play it Allegro and Andante; *p* and *f*.

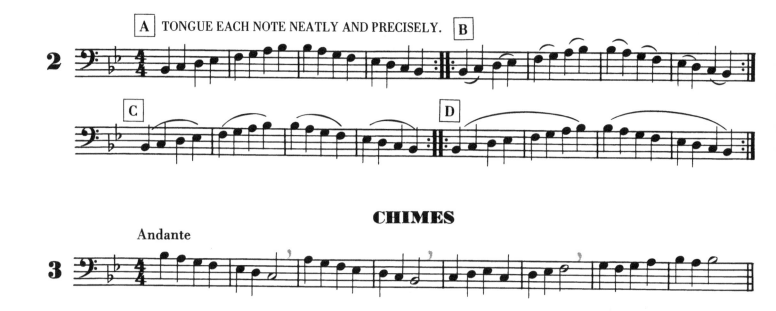

CHIMES

Andante

CRISS-CROSS (Duet)

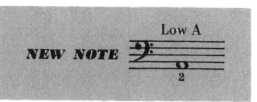

1

MIRROR ECHOES

2

CRUSADER'S MELODY

3

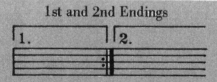

1st and 2nd Endings

When a repeat cannot be shown with the signs learned on page 17, "1st and 2nd endings" may be used. Play from the beginning to the repeat sign :|| in the 1st ending. Return to the beginning (or to the |:). Skip the 1st ending and go without pause to the 2nd ending.

MEXICAN HAT DANCE (Duet)

4

INTERVALS

An *interval* is the distance between two notes. To determine an interval, count the lines and spaces between the notes, beginning with 1 on the lower note.

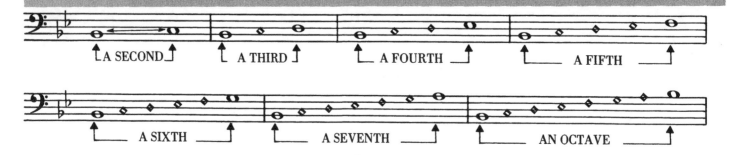

The small, diamond shaped notes above show the steps between the principal notes.

Keep your jaw steady. Don't move any more than is absolutely necessary. Try to hear the note before you play it. Play each note neatly.

1

TAH TAH - - - - - - - - - TOO TAH TOO   TEE   TEE TAH TEE TAH

STUDY IN FORTHS

2

3

YODELING SONG (Duet)

4

Player No. 1

Player No. 2

No. 1

No. 2

22

THE NATURAL SIGN

A *natural* (♮) sign cancels a flat or sharp. If it occurs at the beginning of a measure, all similar notes in that measure are to be played as naturals.

FINGER BUSTER NO. 3

LIP BUILDER NO. 4

BARBERSHOP DAYS (Duet)

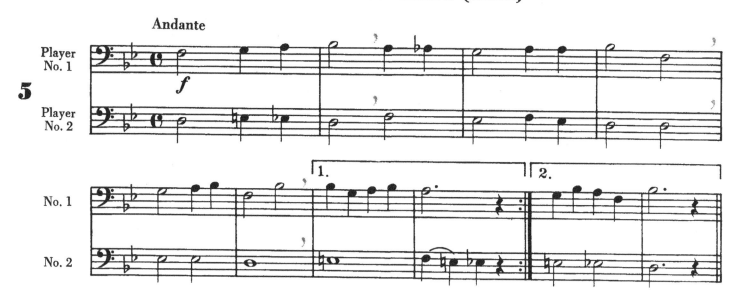

EIGHTH NOTES AND RESTS

An *eighth note* ♪ equals ½ of a quarter note. Two eighth notes can be played in the length of time it would take to play one quarter note. Each beat has two parts; a "down" part and an "up" part.

Start by counting aloud: "1 and 2 and 3 and 4 and." Notice that your foot goes *down* on each number, and *up* on each "and." Now try tapping and thinking the beats. As a last practice before playing, tap lightly, and say softly, "ta-ta-ta-ta, ta-ta-ta-ta." If you can say one "ta" for each down beat and one for each up beat, you are ready to play.

Notice that the arrows show the direction of your foot.   & = "and."

TEN LITTLE INDIANS (Duet)

Mezzo = medium   *Mezzo forte* **mf** *= medium loud*   *Mezzo piano* **mp** *= medium soft*

Train your eye to find the beats in every measure of music *BEFORE* you play. In the pieces that follow, study and think the rhythm before practicing. In this way you will be sure to play the right rhythms. Mark in the "down" and "up" beats as an aid. Learn to recognize and count rhythms as skillfully as you would read a newspaper.

THE CLOCK

EIGHTHS ON ALL COUNTS

MENUET
J. S. BACH

CHANUKAH SONG (Duet)

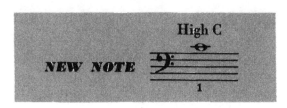

When going higher, remember to think TEE. Start each attack with the tip of your tongue on the back edge of your upper teeth. Don't poke your tongue between you lips!

FRÈRE JACQUES (Round)
(See pg. 13)

FRENCH FOLK TUNE

FINGER BUSTER NO. 4

PLAY No. 4 SLOWLY AT FIRST.
GRADUALLY INCREASE THE SPEED.
ALSO PLAY IT WITH EVERY NOTE TONGUED.

WHEN LOVE IS KIND

ENGLISH

FARE THEE WELL

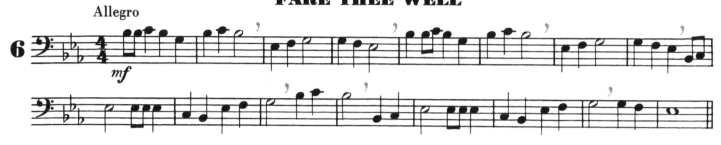

STACCATO AND TENUTO

A *staccato* mark  means to play notes short and detached from each other.

A *tenuto* mark means to play the note to its fullest value.

Simile means to play in a similar style as before.

THEME FROM THE "ACADEMIC FESTIVAL OVERTURE"

J. BRAHMS

Go back to "Chanukah Song" (No. 5 on page 25). Mark in staccato and tenuto indications where they seem appropriate.

AMARYLLIS

GHYS

B FLAT MAJOR ETUDE

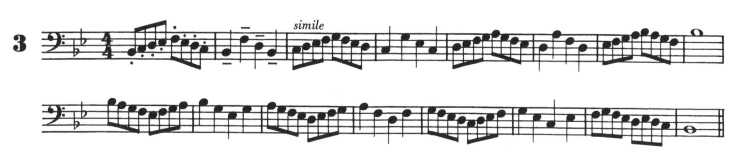

STUDY IN THIRDS

Go back to pg. 22. Can you see how this piece got its name?

PLAY ALL OF
No. 4 USING
EACH OF THESE
VARIATIONS.

MORE DYNAMICS

Crescendo ———————— = gradually louder .   *Decrescendo* ———————— = gradually softer.

The use of crescendo and decrescendo on long tones is very important in developing a firm, clear tone quality. Keep the pitch of each note very straight. Try to support your tone with a large breath. Tense your abdomen as though you were pushing out against a belt that was too tight. Keep your jaw and throat relaxed. Use these long tone studies, and the "Lip Builders" as warm-ups before playing exercises and songs.

SOME PUZZLES IN RHYTHM

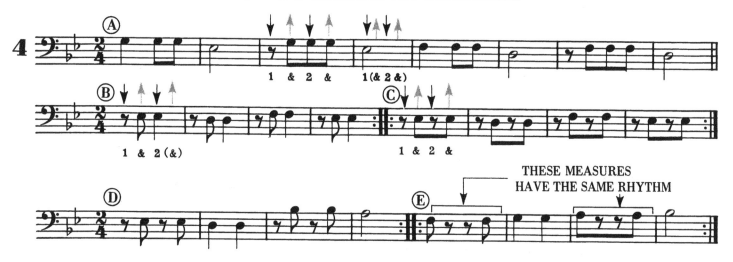

THEME FROM "FINLANDIA"

J. SIBELIUS

THE DOTTED QUARTER AND EIGHTH NOTES

ALMA MATER

AMERICA

CAREY

WE GATHER TOGETHER (Duet)

DUTCH

An *accent*, $>$ indicates that the start of the note is to be emphasized.

MAIN THEME – SYMPHONY NO. 7

SCHUBERT

DOWN THE MAIN STREET

C.F.G.

PARADE OF THE TIN SOLDIERS

LEON JESSEL

SHEPHERD'S HEY (Duet)

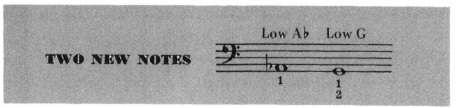

TWO NEW NOTES

Low Ab   Low G

1

Ab   G

LIP BUILDER NO. 5

2

mf — *simile*

Ab

MORE TEMPO MARKINGS

LARGO — Slow and broad; ALLEGRETTO — A little slower than allegro but not quite as slow as moderato. No tempo marking has an exact meaning. A composer tries to give a *general idea* of the speed of the music. Sometimes he will try to be more definite and will show how many beats are to be played in one minute by giving a "metronome marking." A METRONOME is a machine that clicks at different speeds to help the player find the exact tempo.

♩ = 60 means that the speed is sixty quarter notes per minute.

♩ = 120 means one hundred twenty quarter notes per minute.

BLOW THE WIND SOUTHERLY

Allegretto ♩ = 112
sprightly

3

mf

Largo ♩ = 40

4

p

ALL MEN WILL BE BROTHERS (Duet)
(From Symphony No. 9)

BEETHOVEN

Allegro ♩ = 126

5

f

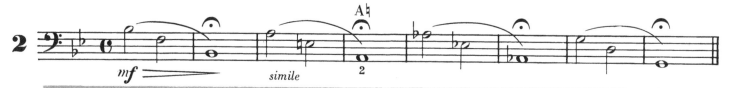

LARGO FROM SYMPHONY NO. 9
(New World)

A. DVORAK

The tie across the bar line makes this Ab also.

MORE TIES

THINK: 1(& 2 & 3)& 4 &

GERMAN FOLK SONG

THESE MEASURES SOUND THE SAME

ZING, BOOM!

CARROLL

Arch Your Tongue. Think of "Tee"

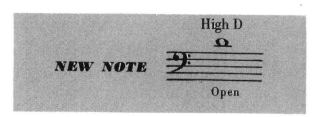

NEW NOTE — High D, Open

It is important to rest frequently when working in the higher register. If your tone sounds forced, STOP. Try again when your lips have rested.

1

Study the construction of the major scale again (pg. 22). If the 1st, 3rd, 5th and 8th steps of the scale were sounded together, a *chord* would be formed. You cannot play chords on your instrument. However, you can play the notes of the chord one after the other. The result is a *broken chord* or *arpeggio*.

Steps of the scale. Notice that both Bb's are called 1 and both D's are called 3.

2

Bugle calls are constructed only on the notes of a chord. An example is. . .

REVEILLE

3

LIP BUILDER NO. 6

4

TEE-OO   TAH   TEE-OO

CAN CAN

OFFENBACH

5

JOLLY OLD ST. NICHOLAS (Duet)

6

Player No. 1

Player No. 2

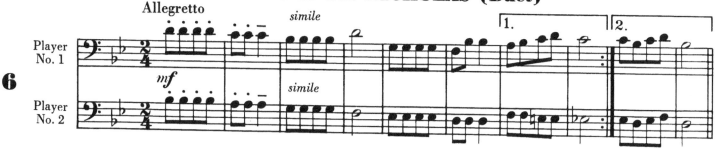

D.C. AL FINE

Da Capo, (D.C.) means to go back to the beginning of a piece of music.

al Fine, means to end at the measure marked *"FINE"* (pronounced FEE-NAY).

MUST I THEN

GERMAN FOLK TUNE

TWO NEW NOTES

Gb MARCH

LIP BUILDER NO. 7

SAD COLORED LEAVES

CARNIVAL OF VENICE

A *sharp* (♯) raises the pitch of a note one half step. A sharp placed before a note affects all notes on the same line or space which follow in that measure.

F Sharp

NEW NOTE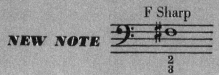

OH LITTLE TOWN OF BETHLEHEM

ENHARMONIC TONES

Notes can have the same pitch but different letter names. They are called *enharmonic tones*. The following chart shows some notes that are fingered the same, sound the same, yet have different letter names. Compare this to homonyms.

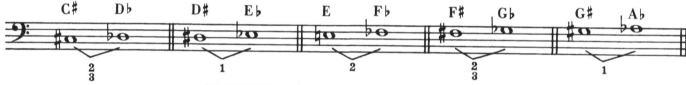

POINT AFTER TOUCHDOWN

Allegro

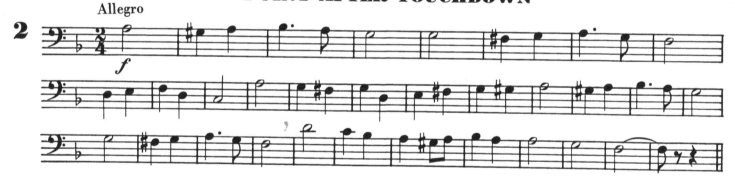

THE GLOW WORM

LINCKE

Ritard, or rit. - - - means to slow down gradually.

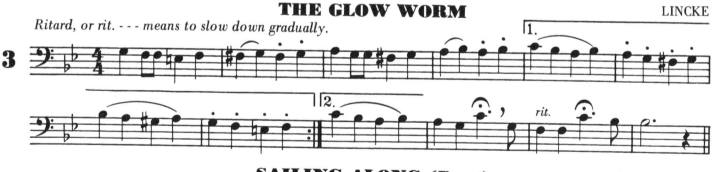

SAILING ALONG (Duet)

Allegretto

C.F.G.

THE A♭ SCALE

1 = whole step
½ = half step

LOW A AND D ARE FLAT ALSO.

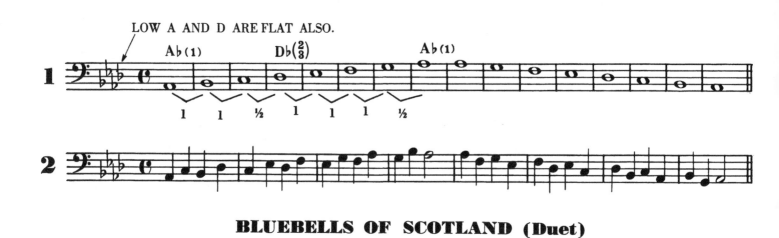

BLUEBELLS OF SCOTLAND (Duet)

Moderato

FINGER BUSTER NO. 5

Start slowly. Gradually bring
the tempo to Allegro ♩ = 120

JOHN PEEL

ENGLISH FOLK SONG

Allegretto

* *a tempo* means to return to the original speed of the piece.

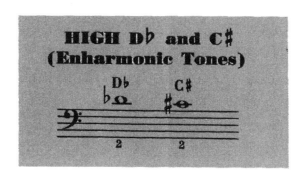

HIGH D♭ and C♯ (Enharmonic Tones)

1

THE SINGING BARITONE

C. F. G.

2 Andante

3 Allegretto

STACCATO STUDY

4

TRUMPET TUNE (Duet)
(ARRANGED FOR BARITONE)

CLARKE

5 Allegro

Player No. 1

Player No. 2

No. 1

No. 2

CUT TIME (Alla Breve) ¢

So far, all time signatures have had the quarter note as the unit of beat.

The sign ¢ shows that all measures have two beats and that a *half note* gets one beat. Cut time may also be written $\frac{2}{2}$

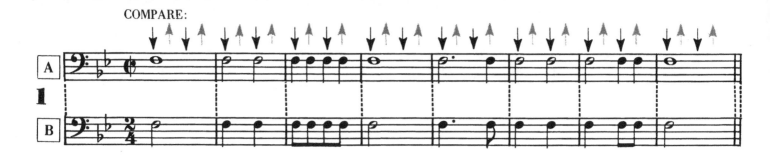

The two lines of music, A and B, are the same when heard. They are quite different when seen. Make sure that you look very carefully at time signatures from now on.

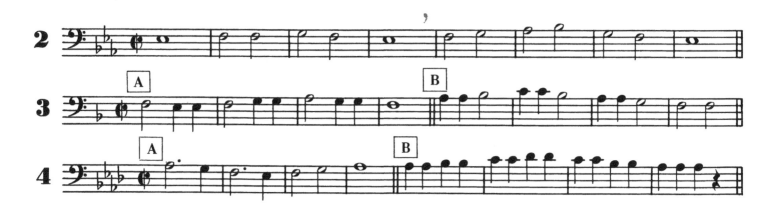

STARS AND STRIPES FOREVER

J. P. SOUSA

SOME RHYTHMIC PUZZLES IN ¢

1

GOOD KING WENCESLAS

2

MANHATTAN BEACH MARCH

JOHN PHILIP SOUSA

3

WHEN THE SAINTS GO MARCHIN' IN (Duet)

4

$\frac{6}{8}$ TIME (Compound Meter)

There are two ways to count $\frac{6}{8}$ time: 6 beats to the measure with an eighth note receiving one beat *or* 2 beats to the measure with 3 eighth notes (or its equivalent) receiving 1 beat.

Slow songs are usually counted *6 beats to a measure* while marches are counted *2 beats to a measure*. Start by counting 6 beats to a measure. Place a slight accent on beats 1 and 4 when tapping and counting aloud.

HEY DIDDLE DIDDLE

TRADITIONAL

LORD LOVELL (Duet)

When you give a slight accent to beats 1 and 4, you probably felt that a new rhythmic pulse was present. This new pulse is $\frac{6}{8}$ counted *2 beats to the measure.* Go back to 1A through 1J. This time, tap 2 beats in each measure and think the rhythm within the parenthesis.

TWO B NATURALS AND TWO C FLATS

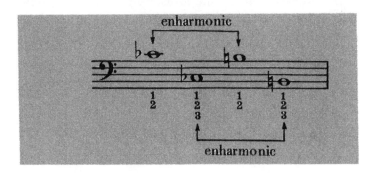

The low C♭ (or B) may sound too high in pitch. This is quite normal, even on the finest instruments. It may be necessary to extend your third valve slide a little to play these lower tones in tune. Ask your teacher about this.

THE C MAJOR SCALE

STUDY IN C

A Triplet is a group of three notes played in one beat. Ⓐ and Ⓑ should sound alike.

PILGRIM'S CHORUS

R. WAGNER

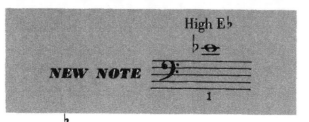

NEW NOTE High Eb

1

Eb MAJOR SCALE

DOES THE FORMULA
FOR MAJOR SCALES
HOLD TRUE HERE?

2

Eb CHORD STUDY

3

This old carol changes meter in the middle. The speed of the quarter note at ¢ is one half the previous dotted quarter in 6/8. See if you can think quickly so that there is no tempo change.

WASSAIL SONG

4

Allegro

1 (& a)   2 &

POMP AND CIRCUMSTANCE (Duet)

EDWARD ELGAR

5

Stately

SIXTEENTH NOTES

A quarter note in $\frac{2}{4}$, $\frac{3}{4}$, or $\frac{4}{4}$ time can be divided into four SIXTEENTH NOTES. Before playing the first exercises, count aloud the divisions shown under No. 1. Keep steady. Make the Sixteenths fit a firm tempo.

BACK AND FORTH (Duet)

LEARN BOTH PARTS
KEEP THE QUARTER NOTE FULL

POLKA DOTS

EIGHTHS AND SIXTEENTHS

KEEP ALL SIXTEENTHS
NEAT AND BOUNCY.

OLYMPIC FANFARE (Duet)

44

VILLAGE POLKA

POLISH FOLK TUNE

1

GRANDMA GRUNTS
(A Rhythmic Puzzler)

APPALACHIAN FOLK TUNE

Allegretto

2

FINGER BUSTER NO. 6

Slowly at first!

3

SKIP TO MY LOU

4

THE DOTTED EIGHTH AND SIXTEENTH

PLAY THE SIXTEENTH NOTE AS IF IT
BELONGED TO THE FOLLOWING NOTE.

5

JOY TO THE WORLD (Duet)

G. F. HANDEL

Allegro

6

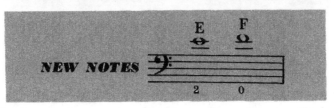

NEW NOTES

These tones are considered optional. If force is necessary to produce them, it is better to wait until endurance and support increase.

F MAJOR SCALE

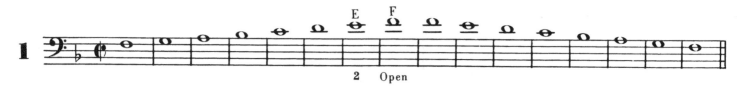

1

LIP BUILDER NO. 8

2

SYNCOPATION

When the accent is placed on the upbeat, it is called *syncopation*.

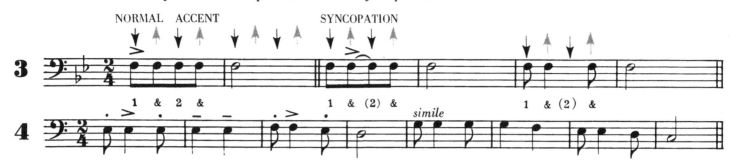

3

4

CALYPSO HOLIDAY

CARROLL

5

GLEE REIGNS IN GALILEE

6

SYNCOPATION IN ₵

Ⓐ and Ⓑ should sound the same.

7

VIVE L'AMOUR

(In 2)

Allegro

CHROMATIC SCALES

A CHROMATIC SCALE is one that is made up entirely of half steps. Notice that sharps are used ascending, and flats descending. Play the scale tongued and slurred.

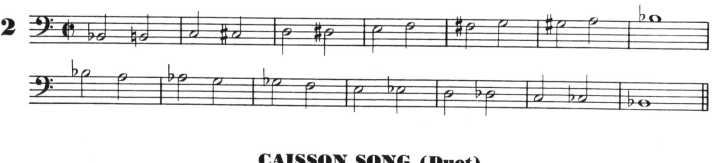

CAISSON SONG (Duet)

March tempo

REVIEW OF SCALES

FINGERING CHART
(for reference only)

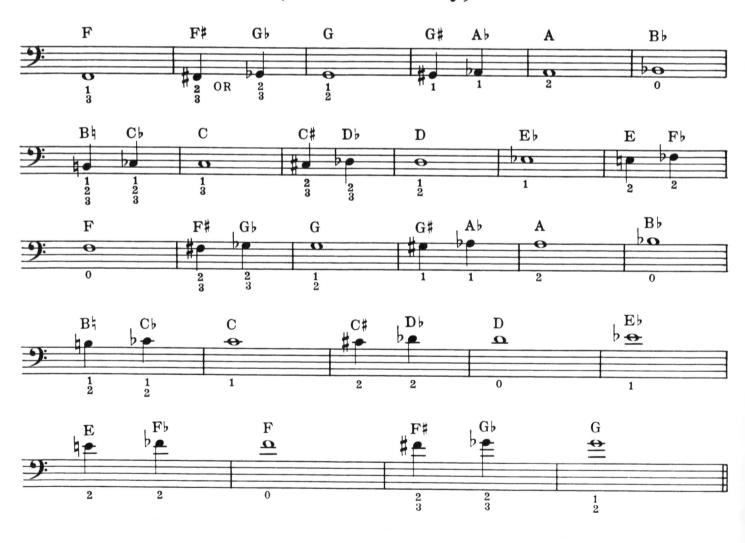